The Principle Woods™
Book of Honesty

Author
Jennifer Whitlock

Illustrator
Kevin Shore

Principle Woods, Inc.
One San Jose Place, Suite 11
Jacksonville, Florida 32257
www.principlewoods.com

Designed by David Whitlock, Principle Design Group, Inc.

0701-01ED

ISBN 0-9700601-6-5

Printed in Singapore

This book belongs to

_____

Dedicated to my editor, Sandy,
who so generously shares her
knowledge, support, and especially, friendship.

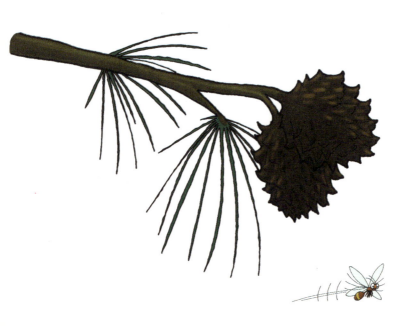

Contents

Principle W

The Beavers' Dam

Great Pine

Grand Oak

Stinky Stump

Sweet Bunnies Burrow

Summertime Blue Juicer Tree

ᎧᎧds

Busy Beaver Creek

Fallen Maple

The Magnolia Clearing

The Cave of Courage

The Honesty Tree

Blossom's Clubhouse

Hidden Pond

Introduction

Growing just this side of the Land of Out There
is Principle Woods, a magical woodland of
beautiful, shady trees; busy, babbling brooks; lush,
green meadows; and more importantly, won-
drous and unique animals.

First you must meet Tipper, a speedy
little squirrel from Great Pine. He's the
first animal to scamper for fun, take a dare, or run a
risk. He's silly, zany, and usually a bit reckless. But,
if you're looking for fun, Tipper will *never* let you
down.

Next we have Springer from Sweet Bunnies
Burrow. To a chubby bunny like him, there's
nothing better than having a good
time. Of course, work occa-
sionally gets in the way of that, and
Springer *does* so hate to work…except
to work a little mischief!

Burly, the broad-shouldered, big-bel-
lied bear from Cave of Courage, cheer-
fully watches over all the animals!

Then, of course, we have the wise owl, Sage. From her perch high in Grand Oak, she protects the forest animals as best she can from the dangers of Out There. It's her wisdom that brings out the best in the others.

Chopsie, a hardworking beaver from Busy Beaver Creek, also tries to bring out the best in others, though her way is much different. She bosses and demands, forcing the forest friends to do what she says. Work, work, work is what she's all about.

Grinder, another hardworking beaver, is Chopsie's best friend. But unlike Chopsie, he's used to accepting orders, not giving them. It's easy to send Grinder into a nervous tizzy, whiskers quivering and tail thumping.

Last, but most *definitely* not least, there's Blossom, the skunk from Stinky Stump. With her moody temper you never know what to expect—a day of grand plans at her clubhouse, fierce scowls and bossiness, or more showing off. No matter what, you can bet there will be adventure!

Welcome to Principle Woods!

Season Switcher

Chopsie was trying to concentrate on her dam repairs, but all she could hear was the sound of Tipper's squirrel-ish chatter ringing in her ears. This was the squirrel's latest game—finding out *just how crazy* he could make her. Finally, Chopsie wheeled around and cried, "Tipper, PLEASE BE QUIET! I am *trying* to concentrate here! Do you know what happens if this dam breaks? Do you? Water would be everywhere, Principle Woods would be swept away. It would be a disaster, I tell you, a disaster! NOW SCAMPER AWAY, SQUIRREL! I must get on with my *work*!"

Tipper just giggled. He started to work on a new chatter-song to further annoy Chopsie when—oh my!—he noticed she was holding an acorn, a lovely acorn, a *lovely*, *superb*, *marvelous* acorn. It was the yummiest of yummies—a warm caramel color and perfectly, wonderfully ripe—and Chopsie was just about to place it right in the center of the dam.

"Wait!" Tipper shouted. "No! Don't use that for the dam! *Obviously*, it's meant for me—only a squirrel could really appreciate, could truly understand, could really love an acorn nibble-snack like that! You must, you must, indeed you *must* get a rock instead and give that beautiful gem of an acorn to *me*! I have never, never, never, nope, nope, nope,

never seen one one like that and I want it, yes, yes, yes I do!"

Chopsie turned to Tipper, narrowing her eyes thoughtfully. "What? *This*? You'd like *this*? Hmmm…you know, I'd love to give it to you, but you see, it seems to be the perfect size to fill this gap in the dam, this one *right here*, and I need it to finish the dam. Well, I'm ever-so-sorry,  Tipper. Perhaps if you weren't so busy chattering my ear off, you could find a few of these squirrel-scrumptious, acorn-tasties yourself."

"You…you aren't going to give it to me?" Tipper asked in disbelief. Who did this beaver think she was, refusing him this wonderful, amazing, *made-just-for-him* acorn?

"No, I am *not* going to give it to you! I'm quite sure you can find an acorn of your own. Indeed, I'm sure there are many just a scurry and a scamper away," Chopsie firmly replied.

Tipper was very upset. "You just wait, waddley old beaver. I don't want any of the other acorns. I *want* that one, and I *will* have it—just you wait!"

The next morning Tipper got an early, early start. Dawn was *just* beginning to break over the forest, the hazy light of the morning sun gave everything a pinkish-orange glow. The squirrel scurried from treetop to treetop until he reached Busy Beaver Creek. Slowly, slowly, *slowly* and carefully, carefully, *carefully*, he began to inch-step over the dam, one paw after the other. At the middle he lay on his belly and *leaned* over as far as he could to reach the acorn— *his* acorn! Working very hard, he closed his eyes and grabbed hold. He started to tug… but…wait…something was very, *very* wrong. Acorns are smooth and round and lie still but…well …this one was furry and it was tugging back! *Furry and tugging?* It wasn't possible…what *was* this thing he was grabbing? He opened his eyes instantly when he heard, "AHA! You little scoundrel! I caught you red-pawed!

Do you know what could have happened if you took this? This one little acorn, this teeny acorn, could very well be the one holding the *whole dam* together! A full flood, Tipper, a *full* flood is what you could have caused by taking it! The acorn was placed right here for a *reason*, Squirrel. Your nasty squirrelly-squirrel greed could have broken down the *entire dam*!"

The story about Tipper trying to steal the very acorn that could be holding the dam together spread quickly through the forest. None of the animals wanted anything to do with Tipper anymore for fear he might take something from them also. Blossom, especially, had stinging words to

share when Tipper wanted to play in her clubhouse. "What? Play with you? Have a sneaky little
squirrel robber over to my *clubhouse*? You must be
joking! I cannot, will not, simply *won't* trust
someone who takes what belongs to someone
else!"

All the animals began to ignore Tipper. It was
lucky that Season Switcher Day was coming soon,
because on that day *everyone* played together.

Season Switcher Day was a delightful, significant day celebrated four times a year in Principle Woods. During each celebration, the Season Switcher Stone was brought out to show when each season would end and the next would begin. Without it, the forest wouldn't know when it should change from one season to the next and how to prepare for the change. The snow wouldn't know when to fall, the trees wouldn't know when to bloom, and the crickets wouldn't know when to chirp—it would be complete confusion!

To just anyone, the Season Switcher Stone might seem like a boring old rock, good

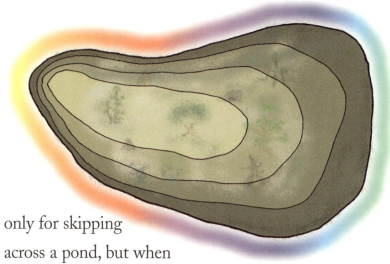

only for skipping
across a pond, but when
the forest friends studied it, they saw something
magical, something mystical. The stone showed a
picture of the forest, a dim, hazy picture. As
spring faded to summer, everything in the picture slowly turned from a vivid, kelly green to a
deep, dark, forest green. Toward the end of summer, when it was time for the Season Switcher
Day celebration, the animals could see the
summer green turning to a pumpkin-like orange;
and then when autumn changed to winter, oranges,
browns, and yellows faded into a
crisp, sparkling white. Season
Switcher Day was not just the
kickoff of a new season, but also a
day of great festivity and fun.

"Yippee! Today, today, today I will get to *play*! Season Switcher Day, here I come!" Tipper shouted. "Today I'll get to play with my friends, yes, yes, yes I will, because *nobody's* angry on Season Switcher Day, indeed, indeed, and indeed they *are not*!" The squirrel just couldn't wait, so with great fistfuls of acorns and nuts, he scampered to Grand Oak. He was the first to arrive, but the others soon followed. Each scorned Tipper in his or her own way. Blossom ignored him by tossing her head the other way whenever Tipper caught her eye; Springer snubbed him by quickly glancing away, pretending to think about something very seriously as he tugged his thinking ear; and the beavers dismissed him by turning away with sharp thumps of their heavy tails.

As was the tradition, Burly had the important job of keeping the Season Switcher Stone safe in his knapsack until it was time for the celebration.

When the great bear arrived, all the animals crowded
around him, "Well? Well? Hurry up! I don't see what
the delay is; I don't see why we have to wait! Get out
the Season Switcher Stone!" Blossom nagged in her
Blossom-ish, pouty way.

"Really, Burly, we've waited enough; now, let's go!"
Chopsie ordered in her Chopsie-ish, bossy way.

Burly enjoyed teasing them by going about the
Season Switching slowly, but when Sage gave him a
quick peck on his head, he knew it was time to get
busy. He pulled his knapsack closer, opened it,
pushed in his paw, and began to grope around for the

stone. He fumbled and felt and rifled through the bag and found…nothing. Absolutely nothing!

"What's wrong, Burly, what's the matter? Did it chip? Did it break? Oh no! We *are* going to switch seasons, aren't we? Oh dear, oh dear, oh dear, we aren't going to be stuck in this season forever, are we? Are we? And the dam—what about the dam? It's the most important part of the switch. How will we know if we're running out of time in order to get it ready for the next season?" Grinder cried anxiously, his tail thumping the ground wildly.

"I'm sure it's in here *somewhere*. Hold on, Grinder, hold on," Burly answered reassuringly.

But even after more rummaging around, he *still* found nothing. The animals held their breath as he shook, shook, shook the bag; twisted it this way and that, and finally turned it inside out.

"It's just gone. I never take the Season Switcher Stone out; I simply don't understand what's happened to it."

Chopsie had a thought. "Hmmm…I hope nobody's *taken* it," she said with a pointed look at Tipper. "I hope nobody here would be as dishonest as *that*."

"What?! You don't think…you couldn't *possibly* think I took the Season Switcher! Surely you know, of course, of course, that I wouldn't do that. I would never take something like a *Season Switcher Stone*!"

"Ha! But you *would* take an acorn that Chopsie told you was absolutely necessary to hold the dam together!" Blossom reminded him. "This isn't a *bit* different! Are you having fun at our expense, Tipper? Is this one of your jokes? Are you getting us all worried just to yell, 'Ha-ha, *I* have the Switcher Stone, yes, yes, yes indeed I do!'"

Tipper was incensed. "I did *not* take it! I did *not*! *When, how, why* would I take it? You believe me, don't you, Burly?"

The bear looked away. It was very difficult to believe Tipper, especially since he had a reputation for taking things that belonged to others.

"I say we search his hollow!" Blossom yelled.

"But Blossom, we can't search his hollow until we have proof he did it!" Springer said, feeling sad because his buddy was in big trouble.

All heads turned toward Springer. Suspiciously, Blossom said, "Oh *really*, Springer? Perhaps *you* took it? Perhaps you know a little more about it than Tipper?"

"Alright, everyone, alright," Sage interrupted before they could go any further. "Suspicious thoughts and accusing words won't help us. We have to find that Switcher Stone because the season

switch *must* be made, and soon! Now, off you go.
Everyone go in a different direction and look hard.
Concentrate." The next few days were spent in an all-
out, full-fledged, top-to-bottom search of the woods.

The weather began behaving quite oddly; bitterly
cold one day, balmy and sunny the next. Some trees
were covered with frost, some with colorful, vivid
blooms, and some with gorgeous fall foliage. The
forest was a mess.

Finally the animals heard shouts of glee ringing
through the woods. Blossom had found the
Switcher. "I found it! I found it! The Season
Switcher Stone is back! Everyone to the clubhouse
for a belated Season Switcher Day celebration!"

All the animals gathered at the clubhouse where Blossom sat waiting triumphantly. As the animals neared, she waved her hands, wriggled her hips, and shook her head from side to side, saying in an I'm-Better-Than-You-Are tone, "No, no, please, hold your applause. Really, it was no problem. Of course, not *everyone* would think to look on the creek island, so please, don't be ashamed that you didn't find it. Really, let's just have the party…no thanks are necessary."

Angry and frustrated, Tipper replied, "Just have the party, Blossom? Oh, I don't *think* so, dear skunk. I, for one, would like to know exactly how you knew to look all the way out on that island. It seems rather odd, a little weird, a little out of place, that you were so positively accusing *me*, but yet *you* were the one to find it! Maybe just trying to throw everyone off your trail? Was that it?"

"Of course not! Personally, I think you put it there after you took it. Don't you agree, Chopsie?"

"No, Blossom, I think perhaps you were right before. I think Springer might have been our dishonest, conniving culprit this time!"

"Oh! No, really, please, I didn't!" Springer exclaimed. " You can't blame me! I had nothing to do with...."

Suddenly Burly bellowed, "If you would all just *hush* a moment, I have something to say! Tipper didn't take the Season Switcher Stone, and neither did Springer, and neither did Blossom. It was *my* fault, entirely my fault."

"WHAT?! Are you kidding? Have you not *noticed* what a mess this forest has been, the trees, the crickets, the weather, even the *Zippers*, have been confused! What is this? A cute little bear-ish joke, perhaps?" Blossom cried, raising her voice after each question.

"It is *not* a joke, Blossom! It was just an acci-dent. As soon as you said you found it on the creek island, I remembered what I had done. Last time I was there, I lay down to have a quick nap after my lunch. I wanted to use my knapsack as a pillow, but the Switcher Stone made it so uncomfortable, so bumpy and lumpy, that I took it out. I just forgot to put it back. That's all. *Case solved*.

However, that's not what's important now. What's important is the way you're all behaving. 'You did it!', 'No, you did it!', 'No, you!', 'No, you!' You should be ashamed of the way you're treating each other. And to think, all this distrust came about from *one* mistake, *one greedy mistake* that Tipper made. Just look how far it's spread; look at the damage it's done."

Recognizing the truth in what he was saying, the forest friends were staring at the ground as Burly spoke. When he finished, they looked up, glancing at each other timidly, unsure of what to say or do next. Then they heard Sage say, "My animal friends, I have an idea." Everyone looked up and saw her perched on the clubhouse door. They hadn't even realized she was there. "Today is not only Season Switcher Day, it's Clean Slate Day as well. Everyone gets a fresh record and a clear, spanking clean conscience! Then *next* Season Switcher Day, the animal who has been honest—*completely honest*—wins a prize.

And, my dears, this is a prize I promise you'll all want to win, yes, it's one I'm *sure* you'll want to win."

The Honesty Tree

Of all the little glens, nooks, and crannies in Principle Woods, each forest friend has a place that is *especially* important, one that is *their Special Spot*. Special Spots are where the animals go by themselves to be bother-free and have a bit of quiet and rest.

The tree where she was born was the place Sage called her Special Spot. It was also a wonderful place for the beavers to visit, although they would never, *ever* dream of disturbing the wise owl if she were spending time there. Undoubtedly, the tree was a beaver's dream with its strong, thick branches; wide, green leaves; and delicate pinkish-bluish blossoms. Nobody could argue that it was *the* most beautiful tree in the forest—an *excellent* tree, a *fantastic* tree, *the perfect tree*!

Whenever the beavers visited Sage's tree, the last thing Chopsie always said was, "Remember, Grinder, this is *Sage's Special Spot.* Don't disturb her when she's here and never, never even *think* of cutting it—promise me!"

Grinder always promised of course, but still, this warning always set him to thinking, "*Why* can't we cut the tree? Wouldn't Sage see, wouldn't she understand, that the tree's branches would be just perfect for the dam? And really, how much of a bother would it be for Sage to find another Special Spot?

After all, she *is* a wise owl. *Surely, surely* she could find another perfect tree."

One afternoon, Grinder sat beneath Great Pine and told Tipper all about Sage's tree. "I don't understand. There must be some other reason—some *secret* reason—why we can't cut the tree. Do you think (and here his voice quavered nervously) that something horrible would happen if the tree were cut down? Maybe, oh my *goodness*, oh *dear*, maybe the forest floor would split right open and swallow us up, Tipper! Oh dear, oh dear, oh dear, I just *know* it's something awful! I'm not going anywhere near it ever, ever again. I won't even look at it!"

The little white tip of Tipper's tail trembled with excitement as he leaned in and whispered in a scheming, naughty sort of voice, "I think, indeed, indeed, indeed I do, Grinder, that you have a responsibility to find out why it's so important not to cut the tree! Yes, yes, yes indeed—you have a responsibility to the other animals to *solve the tree mystery!* You and Chopsie are the only two animals who can cut that tree, and we both know that *Miss Chopsie* would never do it. How about if you *nibble* it, not cut it down, so we can get just an idea of what happens? Just to warn the animals of course, that's the only reason, yes, yes, the only reason. It's for our *protection*—surely you see, surely you understand!"

"I...I don't think so, Tipper. I...I promised Chopsie I wouldn't. No, no—it's Sage's *Special Spot*. I just couldn't disturb it," Grinder replied doubtfully.

"Are you *sure*, Grinder? Everyone will think you are ever-so-brave if you learn the reason the tree shouldn't be cut, if it's dangerous. Why, you'd be a

hero! And I *know* you remember from when you saved Busy Beaver Creek how absolutely wonderful it feels to be a hero!"

Yes, Grinder *had* enjoyed being a hero very, very much when he saved the creek. Maybe, just *maybe*, it was worth just a little chop-chop of Sage's tree to have that feeling again—especially if it were for the good of the forest friends. So one afternoon Grinder told Chopsie he was going to look for some extra leaves and twigs for their dam. "I'll be back soon, OK? I promise!

I'm only going to get some things for the dam, really I am, I…I…I promise!"

Chopsie eyed Grinder oddly. "Well, go for goodness sake. You don't have to *promise*. What's the matter with you?"

"Nothing, nothing. I just want you to know what I'm doing, what I'm up to. Nothing's wrong, really! I…I won't get into any trouble, really I won't."

That wasn't true at all. Grinder was actually going to meet Tipper at Sage's Special Spot. They had decided that Grinder would cut just a bit, just a *very little bit*, out of one of the tree's branches. This little bit would—they hoped— be enough to give them a *hint* of what would happen if the whole tree were cut.

As the two friends met, Tipper said excitedly, "Well? Any problems? Any difficulties? See any spies spying? Did you make sure to promise Miss Chopsie you'd stay out of trouble? A promise will work every time, yes, yes, yes!" The squirrel was so giddy, so *tickled squirrel-ish*, about this mysterious tree adventure that he was jumping up and down, and spinning on his tail.

"Um, no, no problems, Tipper…at least, I don't think so…and I was wondering…maybe we could just sort of *shake* the tree to see if anything happens, and not cut it at all." This seemed like a clever idea to the worried little beaver. They could get a clue about the tree, he'd be a hero, *and* he could take the leaves and twigs that fell off the tree back to the dam, which would sort of be keeping his promise to Chopsie.

"No! We decided to cut and cut we will! Now go on—lock on those choppers and grind away!" Tipper yelped, thrilled and all atwitter. Grinder, however, was feeling nervous and couldn't help but wonder why Tipper kept saying 'we'. Certainly, both of them wouldn't be in trouble if he got caught chopping Sage's Special Spot tree.

"Well, here goes," Grinder mumbled as he waddled closer to the tree. But—oh dear—there was a problem. The branches weren't close enough for him to reach. This certainly wasn't like the willow trees on the creek bank, which have branches that hang low,

low,

low—a most superb height for a branch, as far as the beavers were concerned.

Seeing Grinder hesitate, Tipper yelled, "Just chop the *tree*, Grinder! I'll tell you when you've cut too much. Just *go!*" The squirrel rolled his dancing black eyes and thought, "Honestly, Grinder can *really* be such a little chicken beaver sometimes!"

When nothing happened after Grinder chopped an itsy bitsy bit, Tipper became somewhat frustrated. Surely, all those warnings from Chopsie about not chopping down the tree, all those 'Don't you dare!' warnings, *had* to mean that something would happen if Sage's Special Spot were disturbed. Tipper was simply squirrel-aching to find out what!

Grinder continued to chop and worry. "If I just cut a little, little bit, then I've only lied a tiny, tiny bit...I think." Grinder kept *cutting and cutting*. Finally the beaver stepped back for a look at the tree. Horrified, he realized—*oh no!*—he had cut half way through Sage's Special Spot!

Fearful quiver-shake spasms began to shake Grinder's whole body. With a nervous tug of his whiskers he began to waddle-pace about the tree, worrying, fretting, and beaver-whimpering.

Suddenly Tipper spoke up. "Hmmm...well, I guess I better scamper, scurry, and scoot home. You're on your own, beaver buddy! After all, *I* didn't chop that tree, nope, nope, nope, not me—*I* didn't chop it! So off I go!"

Grinder was at a loss—however would he explain this? "Oh dear, oh dear, *oh no!*" he panicked. "What am I going to do? I guess...yes, I guess I should just go home." So Grinder turned and hurried to the creek, hope, hope, hoping the tree wouldn't come crashing down behind him.

A few days later Sage felt she needed a Special
Spot Day. She was weary from her week-long fly-
about, a trip she took several times a season to make
sure the forest friends weren't in any danger from
Out There. A restful day at her tree sounded simply
delightful—quite the thing to restore her spirits.
But *oh*! When she arrived and saw how damaged
the tree was, she was simply *heartsick*. This didn't
make sense. Only Chopsie and Grinder had teeth

strong enough to cut trees; however, hurting someone's Special Spot didn't seem like something either
of them would do.

Sage bowed her head for a moment to collect her
thoughts, then lifted her wide wings and flew to

Busy Beaver Creek. "Hello, dears," she began, her normally patient voice somewhat tempered by exhaustion. "Someone has cut my Special Spot Tree—almost in half as a matter of fact. Do either of you know anything about it?"

Alarmed, Grinder jumped up. "How can I possibly tell her? She'll be so angry and Chopsie will know I broke all those promises. I'll have to say I didn't do it—I'll just have to," he thought, his mind racing. He wondered why one fib just seemed to lead to another and another. "But…surely…telling *just one more* fib couldn't hurt too much, could it? It seemed the only solution to his problem. "It wasn't me! I promise! I promise!" Grinder lied desperately, frantically.

"Well, it certainly wasn't me," Chopsie stated in a matter-of-fact tone.

Sage didn't know whom to believe. *One* of the beavers was being dishonest, there was no doubt about that. "Well," she sighed disappointedly. "I can't make you tell me, but lies always, *always* come out in the end."

Chopsie looked at Grinder angrily when Sage flew away. "Why did you cut Sage's tree?" she asked furiously. Grinder gave no response. He had decided to make *no more promises* and *tell no more lies*, even if that meant keeping quiet altogether.

For days, Chopsie continued trying to get the truth out of Grinder, but she simply could not convince the little beaver to tell Sage what really happened. Eventually she quit speaking to Grinder. The dam repairs began to fall by the wayside since the beavers weren't working together. They just floated listlessly about the creek, Chopsie frustrated and Grinder sad.

Just as they were rising one morning, the beavers heard a loud, long, frightening CRREEAAK. "What was *that*?!" Grinder cried wildly.

"It *sounds* like a tree when it's about to fall! Come on, Grinder—we have to go find out! We're the tree choppers, and it's our responsibility," Chopsie replied firmly. "I happen to think you *just may have* ruined Sage's Special Spot altogether, Mr. Fibs-a-Lot Beaver!"

Both Chopsie and Grinder expected to find Sage's tree lying on the forest floor when they arrived, so they were surprised to find it still standing. However, the tree was *leaning over dangerously* as though it would fall at any moment! All the other animals had gathered to see this dismal sight and to comfort the dispirited owl.

"Well, I demand to know who did this!" Blossom yelled. "Trees don't *fall over* without a reason, for goodness sake. Who did it? Who has something to say? Speak up, speak up!"

It grew very quiet and then a quiet, remorseful voice—*Grinder's* voice— whispered, "I, uh, I might have something I want to say." All heads spun in the little beaver's direction. They were all shocked—all except Chopsie, that is. She just cut her eyes toward Grinder with a shrewd "I knew it!" sort of look.

"I, um, I did it," Grinder continued guiltily. "Chopsie kept saying to never, never disturb Sage's Special Spot tree, and I *promised* I wouldn't and, well, I guess that was the first promise I broke."

There was another loud CRREEAAK, only this time, *this* time, Sage's Special Spot tree moved in the *other* direction, righting itself some. All the animals gasped in disbelief. How was *that* possible? Trees couldn't straighten themselves once they began to fall!

Grinder, however, hardly noticed the tree moving. He forged ahead with his shameful confession. "I wanted to know what would happen if I *did* cut the tree. I...I...I thought it would be something exciting, and I would be a hero for finding out. So I, um, I promised Chopsie I was going to pick leaves and twigs, but instead I went to the tree to chop a little of it, and well, that was the next lie." Again, the tree CRREEAAKED and stood a little straighter.

The forest friends sat perfectly still, waiting to hear more and keeping a close eye on that tree, that unbelievable, *simply amazing tree.* "Then," Grinder said with a deep sigh and long pause, for this was the fib he was *most* ashamed of, "Then I promised Sage that I didn't harm the tree when she asked if I did. That was the third lie. And that's all."

The animals all gasped in surprise and disgust at the thought of such dishonesty. Grinder threw his paws in front of face, wailing mournfully and cowering beneath their angry shouts. "I…I…I'm *so sorry*," he cried over and over.

Sage, however, said nothing. She was noticing that Tipper was *oddly* quiet. Indeed, the squirrel was simply staring up at the sky, his paws stuffed deep in his pockets as he hummed a few bars of his favorite tune. It was as though he wasn't even paying attention. "Tipper, don't *you* have anything to say?" she asked, knowing the mischievous squirrel would normally be loud and accusatory at a time like this.

The group grew silent once more, watching with interest. Tipper's song slowly faded out. His eyes began to dart nervously from one forest friend to the next. "What? Me? No, no, not me. I *promise* I didn't have anything to do with it."

But suddenly…
CRREEAAK…the tree
once again leaned over as
though about to fall.

"Tipper, are you
positive you weren't
involved? You don't want
to tell us anything?" Sage
asked again.

"I already told you!"
Tipper cried defensively.
"I *promised*, and you have
to believe a promise! I
didn't have anything *at
all* to do with that tree, nothing at all, not a bit, not
a bit, nope, nope, *nope*."

Again, the tree creaked and tilted closer to the
ground, frighteningly so this time, straining to stay
upright against its heavy weight. Tipper and the
other animals glanced at it nervously. They were
beginning to understand that there seemed to be a
sort of *pattern*, a reason for this tree's unusual back
and forth movements.

"Tipper!" Chopsie said in a demanding tone, "I suggest you look at that tree, you scampery, sneaky little squirrel of a squirrel! Apparently, dishonesty sends it close to crashing and confessions stand it straight. And just know this: if it falls, many trees will go down with it and you, *dear squirrel*, will be right there with Grinder clearing them up. Now, did you or did you not have anything—*anything*—to do with Sage's Special Spot tree being chopped?"

Again, Tipper protested that he wasn't involved. And again, the tree leaned far, far, *far* toward the ground. It shuddered, it shivered, it quaked, *and it even croaked*. Finally Tipper exclaimed, "OK, OK, OK, OK, and *alright*! Yes! Yes, I told him he should cut the tree…but it was for the *protection* of all of us. I wanted him to be a hero and protect all of you from the dangerous tree. So there you are! I was just trying to help Grinder, yes, yes, yes, *that's* it, I was just trying to help him! And all of you, of course, of course."

When the tree didn't right itself Sage spoke up. "It seems, Tipper, that this interesting tree, this Honesty Tree, doesn't seem to agree that you were trying to

help Grinder. Perhaps you should try giving us the truth?"

"Oh, alright, alright, so it wasn't just for protection! It might have been for a *little* bit of exciting excitement and thrilling thrills," he admitted, but then continued, not willing to give up yet, "But still, it *might* have protected us along the way!"

The squirrel started to scamper up the nearest tree to head for home, eager to get away from this uncomfortable scene, when he felt Chopsie's paw snatch him. "OH NO YOU DON'T! *You* are not getting out of it that easily! *You* are going with us back to the dam, yes you are, to help repair all the damage it suffered while you and Grinder kept up your lies. Dishonesty has consequences, indeed it does, and *you*, Mr. Squirrel-Fibber, are going to find out just how bad they can be. And believe me, this won't be a quick, stuff-a-few-twigs-in fix, either. This is an all work and no play kind of day you'll be having. *You'll* see. Before this day is out, you'll wish you had never, ever gone near Sage's Special Spot. You won't be telling fibs again either,

especially now that we have the Honesty Tree to make sure you tell the truth!"

Trick or Trapper?

"Burly, Burly! Help, help, help and help!"
Tipper cried frantically one fine morning as
he skidded to a stop just outside Cave of Courage.
His paws were flailing in the air as he leapt about,
wailing and shouting. "Springer's trapped in the
meadow! He's trapped! He's trapped! He's
trapped by…ohhh, by a trapper! Yes, yes, yes, the
trappiest of all trappers! What shall we do? We
simply must, must, must save him!"

Burly, the great bear and protector of the forest,
agreed at once to help. "Now, Tipper, what did
you say had trapped Springer? A trapper? What,
exactly, would that be?" he asked as he and the
squirrel started toward the meadow.

Tipper couldn't seem to meet Burly's eyes as he answered this, and he appeared to be smothering a giggle. "Hmmm? What? Oh, um, I didn't get a very close look, I just kept hearing Springer's calls for help— something about being caught and can't get away, I think. Never you mind because I'm sure, oh yes, quite sure we'll find out more when we get there."

When they reached the edge of the meadow, they began to hear Springer's moans and pleas for help. Tipper grasped Burly's paw and whispered frightfully. "Listen, brave, brawny, Burly-ish bear—you must roar—and I mean really roar— the loudest you possibly, possibly, possibly can, to scare away that trapper!"

So Burly let out a great big…

"RRRROOOOAAAARRRR!"

The squirrel and bear waited. And waited. And waited. Nothing happened and Springer continued to wail. How could that huge roar not scare the trapper, Burly wondered?

"Oh my, oh dear, oh my! Perhaps that didn't scare him because he is such a terribly big trapper," Tipper warbled, his voice shaking as though he was frightened.

As Burly continued to roar, he and Tipper crept closer and closer to the tree where Tipper insisted the trapper and Springer were.

Finally Burly whispered hoarsely, "Tipper, we'll have to go rescue him ourselves. I just don't have any roars left to scare the trapper away."

At that, Springer suddenly popped out from behind the tree, arms spread wide. "Surprise!" he shouted with a gleeful giggle and a topsy-turvy flip.

Burly turned to Tipper, who was now lying on the meadow grass shaking with laughter. "We gotcha, gotcha, gotcha! We gotcha! We sure, sure did!" And to Springer, Tipper said delightedly, "See! I told you it would work! Burly just came running right on over, yes he did!"

The great bear looked from Tipper to Springer, then back again. "What…what?" he stammered. "Hmm? I don't understand…I mean…

what happened?

Where did the trapper go?" he asked, his brow furrowed as he tried to figure this out.

"There is no trapper, you silly bear, you funny bear, you fall-for-any-joke-in-the-book bear! There's no such thing," Tipper explained, holding his sides. His tummy hurt from laughing so hard.

"You lied? I won't be able to roar for a week, my throat is so sore, and all for one of your silly prankster tricks? What if something really happens and I need my roaring voice? Hmmm? What then? Well, you can be sure I won't trust you two again. And you just better hope nothing happens, because I won't be there to save you!" Burly turned and stomped back to Cave of Courage, the ground shaking beneath him.

"Oh, please, please, please," Tipper called after him, annoyed that he couldn't see the fun of the trick. "Can't you take a little joke? We weren't really lying, we were just teasing! It was just a joke, right, Springer?"

Springer was busy tugging his thinking ear. The trick had seemed so funny when they planned it. It didn't seem dishonest then, but now, Burly's sad, long face convinced him it had been a bad idea. Hurriedly, Springer hopped toward him, eager to make up for what he'd done. "Don't be mad, Burly, please don't be mad," he pleaded, clutching at Burly's paw as he moved across the meadow. "I'll...I'll make you some flower juice! I'll bring you some Busy Beaver Creek water! Or some sweet, thick honey—surely all of that will make your throat better." Burly, however, just shook him off and continued to walk away, leaving Springer to stare after him.

It wasn't too long after that mean-trick day that the Principle Woods animals awoke to the sound of rumbling thunder and a sky full of storm clouds. The spring rains had arrived, bringing with them the same fierce winds and thunderstorms they did each year.

Tipper's first thought was of Springer. The squirrel knew the bunny's burrow would flood and that he couldn't swim a single stroke. Immediately, Tipper jumped out of his hollow and scurried from tree to tree until he reached Burly's cave, arriving soaking wet, tired, and completely out of breath. "Help…me…Burly!

You have…to…help…me…save Springer!

It's…this rain…

Sweet Bunnies Burrow is…

going to…flood!" he panted.

"Ha!" Burly scoffed. "I'm not falling for that again, Tipper. You can go try your trick on someone else. I have no reason to believe you ever again. Springer's safe and dry in some little nook or hollow, isn't he? You probably think it would be ever-so-funny to drag me out in this weather."

"No, really! I'm not joking *this* time, Burly! You have to help!"

Burly hesitated, noting that Tipper did seem much more sincere this time. Tipper saw that hesitation and, realizing the bear would probably come with him, began to smile in relief. Unfortunately, the bear mistook that smile not as a sign of relief, but as a sign that he was being set up yet again. So, instead of help, Tipper received a resounding "No!"

"What!? You have to help! YOU HAVE TO!"

Burly continued to insist he wouldn't come with Tipper. "Fine! I guess I'm going to save him myself, indeed, indeed, indeedy I am!" Tipper finally exclaimed. "I don't know how I'll do it yet, no I don't. But after today everyone will know that you, Mr. I'm-The-Brave-Bear, are not the only hero in this forest!"

Off he scampered. He had to move very quickly to avoid getting stuck in the gooey mud. Just a few seconds too long in any one spot and down he'd sink with a loud quirrrzzzz. Each time, he had to struggle and push and pull all at once to free himself from the squishy mess. This effort made his whole body strain and stretch and quiver uncomfortably. Loudly, he grumbled, "Dumb mud! Dumb bear! Dumb rains! Dumb non-swimming bunny! Yes...

yes...

yes! All of them! Dumb, dumb, dumb and ever-so-dumb! Well, I'll show them, yes I will!"

However, Burly was only a few paces back, moving through the cover of the trees. He was enjoying this show immensely. He had decided to tag along to find out whether this really was just another dishonest trick. Surely it was but … if this was a trick, then why was Tipper working so hard to get to Springer's burrow? He could just scamper through the trees and go home.

"It must just be that he wants to let Springer know the prank is off," Burly thought. "Yes, that's it. He's just letting Springer know it's off."

Finally, they arrived at the meadow. Tipper shouted, some desperation in his voice, "I'm coming…Springer! I'll…rescue you! Don't…don't worry!" He was completely exhausted from the tough trek through the woods. His arms pumped at his sides as squelch, squerch, squash, he pulled himself along. His beady eyes were focused on his mud-covered feet, willing them to keep moving forward.

Tipper's frantic tone told Burly that this was no joke. Something was definitely wrong. He charged ahead of the squirrel, grabbed a heavy stick, and shoved it down the burrow, trying to make Springer grab hold. The bunny, however, simply would not take it. "Please Springer! All you have to do is grab the stick and hold on! I'll pull you up—it won't be scary at all. You don't have to be afraid."

Then Burly heard Tipper behind him. "Well, if that isn't just the rudest, yes, yes, yes, the *rudest* trick I've ever heard of! Burly, *you* make me so angry! You said you wouldn't help, and I went through a simply horrible, absolutely terrible time to get here. And to think I could be warm and dry at home by now!"

"Never mind that, Tipper," Burly answered curtly. "We have a problem, a serious problem. I can't convince Springer to take the stick, and he's got to! Pulling him up with it is the only way to get him out. We've wasted too much time. He can't swim, and rain is pouring in there fast. Come on, now! You have to talk him into coming out! Do you want to save him or do you want to argue?"

Tipper glowered at Burly. He was still upset with Burly for lying to him, but he realized that the bear was right, and he better do what he said. He softened his voice a bit. "Sprrringgggerrr! Why aren't you taking that stick, bunny buddy, bunny buddy friend of mine?

Come out, come out, come on out so we can play! There are all kinds of things to do at Burly's—that is where we're going, you know." Tipper tagged that last bit on to entice Springer. Surely the bunny wouldn't refuse fun at Burly's.

Once again the stick went down the burrow and Tipper begged and pleaded with Springer to grab hold. A long pause followed and nothing happened. Burly wiggled and jiggled it a bit. He and Tipper waited. Nothing. Finally…finally, Burly felt a tiny tug on the stick. A tiny, soft little tug that slowly grew stronger and stronger. Burly looked at Tipper and smiled a big bear smile. Whew! What a relief it was to pull Springer out of that hole!

Burly swooped up both friends and headed for Cave of Courage. It was then that Tipper remembered to be angry. He started to wiggle wildly in the bear's arms. "I can't believe you said you wouldn't help me but were planning to the whole time! You tricked me! Yes, yes, yes, and *indeed you did!* Do you really think I would have sloshed through all that rain and mud if I knew you were going to help me? And another thing, I—"

Burly cut him off, his bear smile stretching from ear to ear. "What? What's that you say? Lie? I didn't lie. I was just joking when I said I wouldn't save Springer. Surely now, surely you, you of all squirrels, can take a little joke… right?"